ALPHA BILLIONAIRE
PART 2

HELEN COOPER

ALPHA BILLIONAIRE is a three-part novella serial. Thanks for purchasing this book. Please **join my mailing list** to be notified as soon as Part III is out.

Acknowledgments

This is a crazy book, maybe crazier than even I expected it to be. However, I kept it crazy because of the awesome feedback I received from my early readers. All my thanks goes out to Emma Mack my editor, Katrina Jaekley, Stacy Hahn and Tanya Skaggs for reading, proofreading and providing feedback chapter by chapter. I couldn't have done it without you.

And to all the readers, buckle up. It's going to be a bumpy ride. I hope you enjoy the book.

Table of Contents

Prologue 1

Chapter One 3

Chapter Two.. 14

Chapter Three.. 27

Chapter Four.. 32

Chapter Five.. 42

Chapter Six.. 51

Chapter Seven.. 63

Note From Author... 66

Other Books By Helen Cooper... 67

Prologue

"Touch me, tease me, and never leave me,
Kiss me, lick me, I won't think you're easy,
Fuck me, blow me, and close your eyes
I'm going to take you on the ride of your life."

He whispered in my ear as his fingers trailed down my stomach and closer to my panties. "Do you like this, Evie?" His voice was raspy, more urgent and his eyes searched mine. I stared back at him with my heart pounding. I shivered at the look of desire in his eyes. I was in over my head and I knew it. He smiled then, a warm satisfied smile as if he could read my mind. His fingers stopped their journey and he grabbed my hands. "Are you ready for what's next?" He pulled me towards him, not blinking. I nodded slowly, barely believing that I was agreeing to his offer. "Good." He said before his lips crushed down on mine, claiming what was his. I melted against his chest and kissed him back passionately; wanting to be an active part of this journey he wanted to take me on. His hands squeezed my shoulders as he kissed me and I cried out as he pulled my hair roughly. He chuckled at the sound and pulled away from me. "You need to toughen up if you want to do this. Do you understand?"

"Yes." I finally whispered a reply. "I understand."

It was then that I heard the door close. We hadn't been alone.

"He knows?" I looked up at him in confusion, anxiety running through my veins.

"Yes." He stilled. "He knows."

Chapter One

"Don't touch me." I pushed Tyler away from me as hard as I could. He stepped back and stared down at me with a twinkle in his eyes.

"Such a strong push for a girl so..." His voice trailed off and I stared into his eyes searching for some sort of glimmer. All I wanted from him was the truth about Grant.

"Why won't Grant let me leave?"

"Why do you want to leave?" He stared at me disdainfully. "Didn't you enjoy his lovemaking?"

"You're so rude." I shook my head, my face afire with embarrassment. Was he calling me out for sleeping with Grant? "It's none of your business."

"I didn't say it was." He shrugged. "I should leave."

"Where are you going?" My voice dropped. I didn't want him to leave me by myself.

"Out."

"Out? Now?" I grabbed a hold of him. "Take me with you."

"You want to run away from Grant?" He paused and leaned in towards me, his tongue trailing down my cheek for a few seconds. "Or do you just want to be with me?"

"What are you talking about?" I gasped and stepped back, my cheek hot with fire from his touch. "I just want to go home."

"Do you know the story of Little Red Riding Hood?" He asked softly, his eyes intense on me.

"Doesn't everyone?" I rolled my eyes and shivered.

"What was the lesson you learned from Little Red Riding Hood?"

"I don't know. Don't trust people pretending to be your grandma with hairy faces?" I tried to crack a joke to lighten the mood, but he didn't crack a smile.

"No, the lesson to be learned is that Little Red Riding Hood should have been smarter before she even reached the house. She should have realized that anything could have been waiting for her."

"But she got the better of the wolf." I licked my lips. "She wasn't to know that the wolf was a psycho."

"What wolf is not?" He stared at me for a few seconds and I could see him studying my face carefully. "Why did you come back here with him?"

"You don't want to know." I bit my lower lip, feeling ashamed.

"I do." He stared at the rumpled sheets and then back at me. "I very much want to know."

"What's going on?" Grant opened the door and walked into the room, looking at Tyler and me with narrowed eyes.

"We were just talking." Tyler said smoothly. "Do you have a problem with that?"

"Why would I have a problem with that?" Grant looked annoyed and stared at Tyler, who was staring back at him defiantly. I stared at the two men in front of me and swallowed hard. There was Grant looking so handsome and virile. His dark hair shadowed his face and his eyes were intense and possessive as he gazed at me. Then I looked at Tyler, so strong and buff. His blue eyes, light, as they gazed at me with questions. I shivered as I stared at his arms, so strong and muscular. Tyler licked his lips slowly and grinned, a devilish, captivating and spine-chilling grin.

"So Evie." He said softly as he took a step towards me. "What do you say?"

"Say to what?" My heart beat faster as he looked me over from head to toe. What was he asking me? What was going on here? Was this some sick sort of game?

"What do you say to the big bad wolves that are both ready to eat you up?" He whispered into my ear.

"What?" My jaw dropped as I stared at him. Was he saying what I thought he was saying?

"Are you ready to be breakfast?" His husky tone dropped and I felt his hand on my lower back. "Or would you rather be lunch?"

"What?" I repeated, my stomach churning. Was he propositioning me for a threesome?

"Nothing." He laughed and looked back at Grant. "The call go okay?"

"Yes." Grant nodded and his eyes narrowed. "Anything else?"

"No, that was it." Tyler smiled and walked out of the room. I stood there staring at the door wondering about our exchange. Grant and I stood there in silence and when I finally looked at him, he frowned.

"What was that about?" His lips thinned as he surveyed my body. "You seem to be awfully close with Tyler."

"We were just talking."

"Talking about what?" He took a step towards me.

"Fairy tales." I said softly and laughed almost hysterically. I wanted to slap myself to see if this was real. Was this just a bad daydream I'd found myself in?

"Fairy tales." He looked smug. "Am I your Prince Charming then?" He cocked his head. "Or your knight in shining armor?"

"Neither." I bit my lower lip. "You haven't rescued me."

"What do you call the five grand I gave you?"

"You haven't given me anything and I don't want it." I shook my head. "I just want to go home."

"Oh, Evie. Why do you want to leave so quickly?" He walked forward and ran his fingers down my shoulder. "Didn't you have a good time last night?"

"Last night was fun, but that's not who I am. I don't sleep with strange men."

"You slept with me." He leant forward and sucked on my lower lip. "And I think you enjoyed it. Very much."

"I..." I paused, unable to lie as my body responded to his touch.

"Do you want to go back to bed?" His tongue licked my lower lip.

"Why?"

"I'm hungry."

"What?" I froze. "Hungry?" I looked towards the door slowly. Was this a test? Was Tyler about to come back into the room? Were they about to ask me if I wanted a threesome? My face burned as I realized that, while I was horrified at the idea, I wasn't totally against it. A part of me tingled at the anticipation. What would it be like to be with two men? And what did that mean about me? All my life I'd been the good girl. The one boyfriend at a time girl. The no casual sex girl. The only hooking up after three dates girl. Now here I was and all of that meant nothing. I'd had my first one night stand and it had been amazing. The only part that felt bad was my guilt, but I knew that was all on me. That was my good Christian girl shouting at me, telling me that I'd done a bad, bad thing. I didn't want to think that I'd done a bad thing, but I knew that I was in some sort of purgatory in my thoughts.

"For your body." Grant said slowly and then looked at the door. "Are you waiting for something?"

"No, no, of course not. Why would you think that?"

"I don't know." He shrugged. "You just seem preoccupied."

"I just, I don't know. You're acting crazy and I'm wondering if I'm going to be stuck here forever like Sleeping Beauty or Rapunzel."

"Rapunzel?"

"You know. The girl that was locked in the tower and had to climb down her hair?" My voice trailed off. What was I talking about?

"No I don't know her." He grinned. "I don't have a tower here, but I'll see what I can do." He winked at me and pulled me towards him. "I can climb down your..."

Knock Knock.

"Yes?" Grant's voice was annoyed as we both turned towards the door.

"I need to talk to you." Tyler's voice was stiff and he didn't look at me as he stepped into the room again. I tried to avoid looking at him. I wasn't sure why my heart was beating so fast again. There was something about Tyler that I couldn't resist and I didn't know why. It confused me inside. And I was confused and worried enough as it was. I desperately wanted to get out of this house, but for some reason Grant didn't want to let me go. The panic in my head was screaming at me for being so calm. The adrenaline in my veins was telling me to make a run for it. Every fiber of my being was trying to convince me that there was something majorly off in this situation, but I just couldn't seem to step away. A part of me, a part of me that I didn't know existed was captivated by the two men I was with. I was caught up in some sort of spell. A part of me liked the hint of danger that I felt. That was a part of me that I wanted to shake out of me, but I couldn't.

"What do you want?" Grant's voice was frustrated as he looked at me for a brief second. There was unabashed lust in his eyes and my body cried out in remembrance of the previous night.

"We have a problem." Tyler pursed his lips. "We need to talk. Now."

"Fine." Grant let out a huge sigh. "I'll be back."

"Go and have a shower, Evie." Tyler said to me softly.

"What?" I stared at him in confusion.

"Go and have a shower and get dressed." He ordered me as Grant walked out of the room.

"Who do you think you are?" I said softly, not getting why he thought he could boss me around.

"I don't think, I know." He took a step towards me. "If you know what's good for you, you will go and have a shower and put some clothes on."

"Why?"

"Because that way, you don't have to sleep with Grant again."

"What?" My voice rose.

"Everything okay?" Grant looked back into the room. "What's going on?"

"Evie's just telling me what she wants for breakfast." Tyler didn't even look back at Grant. "Go down to the study and I'll meet you there." He looked back at me for a few seconds and I could feel my chest rising quickly as I stared at his face. In this moment, I could see the ex-cop in him.

"Why did you leave the police force?" I asked him softly.

"What?" He frowned.

"Was it because you didn't like having to take orders?" I rolled my eyes. "You seem to think you can just boss everyone around. I'm surprised Grant lets you talk to him like that. You seem so insubordinate."

"You think so?" He grinned at me. That wasn't the response I'd been expecting to receive. His grin surprised me and delighted something in my soul. He was truly in a state of delight at my comments. His eyes were light and almost jumping at me. The smile on his face took me aback. It took him from a serious, hard man to an even more sexy and humorous figure. Why did he have to be so sexy?

"If you were my employee, you'd be fired for the way you talk to me."

"It's a good thing I'm not your employee then."

"I hope that Grant doesn't fire you in the study." I gave him a wide smile, showing him that I meant the opposite of what I said.

"I don't think I have to worry about that." He laughed and ran a finger down my cheek. "If he fired me, I wouldn't be able to do this."

"You shouldn't be doing that anyway." I gasped as we stood there staring at each other. "You shouldn't be touching me."

"Why not?"

"Tyler, I'm here with your boss!" I pursed my lips and stepped back. "You're being highly inappropriate."

"I am?"

"You shouldn't be touching me or propositioning me."

"I've propositioned you?"

"You want to sleep with me!"

"What's wrong with that?" He winked at me and licked his lips.

"I'm not a toy."

"Do you not want to be with me?"

"I'm not that sort of girl. I don't go from bed to bed." I could feel my face heating up. "Imagine if Grant heard you."

"I don't care if he hears me." His eyes narrowed and the smile left his face. "What you did last night was stupid, you know that right?"

"I don't need you lecturing me."

"Why not? Because you have a brain?"

"Excuse me?" I gasped and reached forward to push him away from me. "You're a jerk. What I do or don't do is none of your business." My hand connected with his chest and he grabbed it and pulled me towards him.

"You have no idea Evie. You have absolutely no idea."

"What do you want from me? Is this some sort of game you're both playing with me?"

"I don't play games." His lips came towards mine. "Let me kiss you."

"No." I swallowed and whispered back, my lips a mere inch from his. "You can't."

"I can." He pressed his lips against mine lightly. I felt a sliver of electricity pass from me as his moist lips caressed me. "I can and I will."

"How did Eugenie die?" I whispered against his lips as he pulled back. All of a sudden all I could think about was the girl on the mantelpiece. My body was throbbing. My brain was fuzzy. My skin was on fire. And my heart was thudding. I stared at him and waited for his answer. I wasn't sure why I brought her up as opposed to telling him off for kissing me. Maybe because my lips were still tingling from his touch.

"It's a long story." He paused, his features darkening.

"I've got time."

"It started the way your story started..." His voice trailed off and his eyes darkened, turning from blue to black.

"What do you mean?"

"She went to a club to make a little money." He shrugged. "She fell into the hole."

"What hole?"

"The hole of depravity and sex." He sighed. "Do you know how the tale of Little Red Riding Hood ends?"

"She's saved from the wolf." I said slowly, my heart racing. "The woodsman comes and saves her."

"No." He shook his head, his eyes sad. "That's the rewritten version. In the original version, the French version written by Charles Perrault, Little Red Riding Hood is tricked by the wolf and she ends up being eaten. There is no one there to save her. At the end of the real story, all that is left is a fat wolf."

"What are you trying to say?" I frowned. "What happened to Eugenie? Did Grant do something to her?"

"If I were to tell you I wouldn't be a good employee, would I?" He nodded his head slowly. "And I'm already close to getting fired, as you so delicately pointed out." He stepped back and walked to the door. "Go in the shower Evie. Shower and get dressed." He walked out of the room briskly and I stood there in shock, my body shaking in fear. This was not a joke anymore. I was in serious shit. I closed my eyes and took a deep breath. I needed to find a way to get out of here. And I needed to find it quickly. I certainly didn't want to be anyone's dinner.

Chapter Two

You ever watch those horror movies and watch as the woman runs right into the hands of the villain. You sit there and watch her slowly walking through the house and you want to scream at her to go and hide in a closet or jump into a car or call 911 or do something, other than walk towards the person that's after her. It happens in every horror movie. You sit there with your heart in your hands, your brain screaming at the woman begging her to stop being so stupid. You think to yourself, if that was me, I wouldn't be sticking around or grabbing a small kitchen knife. I'd be hiding or running. It's so easy to watch movies and think that. It's a lot harder to be in a situation of danger, and know what to do.

I'm not stupid. I know that something is off in this house. I know that Grant and Tyler seem like they are bad news. I know I was dumb to come back with Grant after knowing him for barely ten minutes - and even dumber for having sex with him. I know many people would find it hard to believe that I'm not a slut or someone that has casual sex a lot. I don't. And I'm not even sure why not. I don't have anything against casual sex. In fact, I rather enjoyed being with Grant last night; even though I was now starting to question myself.

"Leave, Evie. Grab your clothes and leave." I muttered to myself as I stood there. I couldn't seem to move my feet and I knew that a part of me didn't want to leave. A part of me wanted to find out what had happened to Eugenie. I was an investigative reporter. At least that's what I wanted to be. How could I leave now that there was a real mystery right in front of me? I know, I know. I'm dumb. I should have fled right away. But I was also intrigued by Tyler. And I hated myself for it. It made me feel cheap. I walked to my phone and quickly called Hailey, she'd know what I should do.

"Hey, it's me." I whispered as soon as she answered.

"Where the fuck are you, Evie?" Hailey sounded upset.

"I already told you that..." I started and she cut me off.

"I can't believe that you hung up on me last night." She was fuming. "Where are you?"

"I'm still at Grant's house."

"Who the fuck is Grant?" She screeched.

"The guy I met last night." I said softly. "Look, I don't think I should leave right now."

"Oh my God, do not tell me you had a one night stand and now you think it's going somewhere?" Hailey was shouting. "I knew this was a mistake. Please Evie, just come home."

"Hailey." I walked towards the bathroom so that the two men couldn't hear me. "I don't think a one night stand is going anywhere."

"So you had sex with him?" She screamed.

"Hailey, stop it!"

"Was it good?" She said softly. "I hope it was the best sex of your life because I am going to kill you when I see you."

"It was good, but that's not what I'm calling about."

"What are you calling about?" She sounded suspicious. "Oh God, do not tell me you're pregnant."

"Hailey," I giggled. "I had sex last night, I'm not going to wake up knowing I'm pregnant."

"Evie, I can't believe I'm having this conversation with you." She screeched again. "Tell me about this Grant."

"Well the reason I'm calling has to do with another guy."

"You did not have a threesome." She screeched again.

"Hailey, get a grip." I sighed, though my face warmed at the thought. "You know I didn't have a threesome. You know I don't do threesomes."

"Well, you never did one night stands' either."

"Hailey, non-judgment zone please." I sighed. "I was doing you a favor remember."

"I know, I know. So what's going on with Grant and this other guy?"

"So this other guy was telling me about this girl that died and I think Grant did something to her. I think something fishy is going on."

"Oh God, Evie, get the fuck out of there."

"I think I should stay and try and figure out what's going on."

"Are you out of your bloody mind?"

"I was out of my mind when I agreed to do this job for you." I sighed. "I didn't even get my five grand."

"I'll give you five hundred if you come now." Hailey pleaded. "Please do not go playing Nancy Drew, Evie. You're not Nancy or Veronica Mars."

"What about Stephanie Plum?"

"Evie." She groaned. "Just come home please."

"Grant doesn't want me to leave." I whispered. "At first I thought it was a joke, but I think he might be a bit of—"

"Why aren't you in the shower?" Tyler walked into the room with a frown on his face. I quickly closed the phone and gave him a weak smile.

"I was just calling my friend."

"For?"

"To let her know I was alright."

"So you're alright?" He shook his head. "You're stuck in a house you want to leave, yet you call your friend to tell her you're alright? Are you crazy?"

"No, are you?" I licked my lips nervously. "I'm about to go in the shower now."

"Can I come in with you?"

"No." My fingers trembled and I dropped the phone. Tyler walked over to me and we both bent down to pick it up. As we both grabbed it, our fingers touched and we stopped and stared into each other's eyes. Tyler's expression looked sad as he stared at me and I could see him studying me intently. He reached up and brushed a piece of hair away from my eyes.

"You have beautiful green eyes. They remind me of the night time forest near the house I grew up in."

"Oh?"

"They have a dark green, almost brown hue to them. They're inviting me in, yet I feel something treacherous lurking beyond their beauty."

"You think I'm the treacherous one?" I gasped and he nodded.

"There's more to you than meets the eye, Evie."

"There's really not. I promise." I stood up and tried to grab my phone away from him. "I'd like it back now please."

"Maybe not now. Maybe later."

"What?" I frowned. "Give me my phone back." I grabbed his hand and tried to remove my phone from his grip. My heart was beating erratically and I could feel my face growing cold.

"Sorry." He shrugged.

"Give it back." I squeezed his hand as hard as I could.

"What are you doing, Evie?" Grant walked into the room and stared at us, his expression blank.

"Tyler took my phone and I want it back."

"You took her phone?" He stared at Tyler for a second.

"Wasn't that your order, Sir?" Tyler responded quietly and I saw Grant's eyes narrowing before he looked back at me.

"Come with me, Evie." He held his hand out. "Let's go and talk."

"Talk about what? I want my phone."

"Don't you want to—"

"I don't want anything, but my phone." I pulled away from him.

"What's going on with you?" He frowned, his blue eyes eyeing me warily.

"I want to go home now."

"I told you, that's not a possibility right now."

"Why not?"

"Let her go, Grant." Tyler's voice was soft as he spoke up. "Just let her go."

"No." Grant shook her head. "I'm, I mean, we're not done."

"Done with what?" I swallowed hard.

"Stop asking questions." Grant turned away. "Take her to the room, Tyler. Let her sit there and think for a while." He looked at me for a second and then left the room again. I stood there feeling scared and annoyed at myself. Why hadn't I tried to find an escape when they had both left the room.

"What room?" I shouted nervously and looked at Tyler's blank face. "What room is he talking about?"

"The playroom." Tyler said his expression cool.

"What playroom?" I asked again, desperately wanting to be out of this situation. "Please just let me go home."

"That won't be possible." Tyler shook his head. "Not right now." He grabbed my arm and pulled me towards the door.

"At least let me shower and put some clothes on first. Please." I begged him and he paused. "Please. I don't want to go into another room with just this cover on. I don't want to be naked underneath."

"Fine." He pulled me to the bathroom and opened the door. I walked in eagerly, hoping that I could climb out of the window and escape, but he followed behind me.

"What are you doing?" I froze as he locked the door.

"Letting you shower."

"With you here?" I shook my head, my face red. "I can't shower with you in the room with me."

"It's the only way you're going to be able to shower." He shrugged and leaned against the door. "It's your choice."

"Will you close your eyes?" I asked him softly, my body tense as I stared at him.

"Would you believe me if I said yes?" He grinned and reached forward and grabbed my bathrobe.

"What are you doing?"

"Helping you get ready for your bath." He loosened the belt and paused as the robe fell open. His hand dropped and he stepped back and looked at me, my breasts barely covered by the thin material. "You should shower quickly." He turned away sounding mad at himself. "I'll give you five minutes."

"Five minutes to shower? What?" I blinked at him. "That's not long enough."

"Four minutes and fifty-five seconds left." He looked at his watch.

"Whatever." I reached in and turned the shower on and put my hand out to feel the temperature of the water. "Will you at least turn around please?" I sighed as I felt the water turning warmer. "Please?"

"Fine." He rolled his eyes and turned around. I pulled the robe off quickly and entered the shower, letting the hot water cascade down my body. I wasn't sure why I didn't feel more panicked. I think it was because it hadn't really hit me. The whole situation felt surreal. And if I was honest, a part of me felt safe when Tyler was around. I knew that Grant was his boss and he would follow Grant's orders, but I was also pretty sure he wouldn't let anything bad happen to me. He wouldn't physically harm me. I wasn't sure why I was so confident of that fact, but somehow, inherently I just knew.

"Why are you doing this?" I said as I reached for some shampoo and rubbed it through my hair quickly. My body was on high alert and I felt uncomfortable showering with him in the room, even though I knew he wasn't facing me.

"Why am I doing this?" He repeated. "So you don't try and escape through the window."

"No, I mean, why won't you just let me go. Why won't Grant let me go?" I grabbed the body wash and started soaping my body up quickly, rubbing myself hard.

"What do you want me to say, Evie?" His voice was angry. "I'm just following orders. You should have thought about what you were doing when you got in the car with Grant last night. You should have thought twice before you went to a bachelors' party to strip naked for men. You should have thought twice before you decided to sleep with a strange man. Maybe you should have been asking questions before you made those decisions."

"I know I was stupid." I sighed. "But I was attracted to him and he was nice and it was just going to be one dance."

"Really?" He laughed, an angry sarcastic sound. "You thought you were coming back for one dance?"

"He seemed nice." I bit my lip and turned the water on hotter. "Yes, I was attracted to him. Yes, a part of me thought that it would be fun to hook up. I don't know what I was thinking. I guess I wasn't thinking. I mean no-one expects their first one night stand to be with a psycho."

"Grant's not a psycho."

"Oh okay, sure. He just won't let me leave his house. He's not a psycho at all." I exclaimed angrily and he laughed. "It's not funny."

"I'm not laughing." He said softly and turned around slowly. "I'm not laughing." He said again as his eyes looked at me seriously and I gasped and placed my right hand and arm across my breasts and my left hand in front of my pussy.

"What are you doing?" I glared at him. "You said you wouldn't look."

"No I didn't." He raised his eyebrows and I saw a glint in his eyes as he stared at me. "You asked me to turn around and I did. I didn't say how long I'd turn around for."

"If you were a gentleman, you'd turn back around."

"If I was a gentleman?" He burst out laughing and his eyes crinkled as tears fell down his cheeks. "Oh Evie, what makes you think I'm a gentleman?"

"You're not." I shook my head and then I felt shampoo running into my eyes "Shit." I mumbled. I didn't know which hand to use to brush the shampoo out of my eyes. Either hand being moved would reveal something I didn't want him to see.

"Oh Evie." He sighed and I gasped as he stepped into the shower with me and rubbed the shampoo out of my eyes. "Put your head back." He said bossily and I felt his fingers rubbing my head and rinsing the shampoo out.

"Your clothes are getting wet." I muttered as I blinked at him, standing so close to my naked body.

"I don't care." He muttered and stared at me with a grim smile, his blue eyes dark as he continued to rub my scalp.

"You didn't need to do that." I shook my head and bit my lower lip. He was so close to me. If he moved one inch closer, my naked body would be next to his.

"I didn't want you to have to move your hands and expose yourself." He said with a laugh in his hands.

"Oh." I gasped as his hands fell to my shoulders. "If you had turned back around, that wouldn't have been a concern."

"But what fun would that have been?"

"Why are you flirting with me?" I gasped as his hands rubbed my back, his fingertips massaging my muscles.

"Because there's something about you that I like."

"I slept with your boss last night." I spat out, as much for him as myself. I needed to ignore the heat that was rising up through my stomach. I needed to ignore the sexual tension I felt for him.

"You made a mistake. It happens." His hands ran down to my lower back and stopped just above my ass. "You didn't know then what you know now."

"Tyler." I moved my right hand to push him back.

"Yes?" He grinned and it was then I realized my mistake. He took another step forward and I felt my breasts pushed up against his chest. He looked at me with glittering eyes, his eyelashes filled with water drops. His arms wrapped around my waist and pulled me towards him. I felt his erection pushing up against me through his pants and I held my breath, as his fingers made their way up my body.

"Your clothes are going to get wet." I whispered against his lips.

"As wet as you are right now?" He grinned and my body crumpled against his. I had no resistance towards this man. His fingers made their way to my stomach and we both stood still waiting to see what was going to happen next. I stood there with my body on fire and I had no idea what I was going to do next. He kissed my neck then and I reached out and grabbed his shoulders so I didn't fall. I felt his teeth biting into my skin and my legs trembled at his touch. And then he stepped back and out of the shower. I gazed at him in surprise and disappointment.

"I'm not going to hurt you, Evie." His eyes pierced mine as his fingers ran over the top of his head. "You can trust me."

"I can't do anything with you." I shook my head and closed my eyes, trying to ignore my body's cries. "I don't know why I'm even here and you're not exactly my savior." I tried to remind myself of the situation I was in. "I can't—"

"It's okay." His voice was soft. "I know you're confused. It's okay."

"I'm not confused." I opened my eyes. "I just want to leave."

"You can't leave until the boss says you can."

"What's he going to do to me?"

"I won't let him do anything to you, Evie." His voice was rough. "In every wolf pack, there is an alpha. And in this case I'm the King."

I stood there staring at him and rubbing the soap softly off of my body, imagining it was his fingers touching me. I shivered as he stood there staring at me with a closed off expression. What was Tyler talking about? What was he going to do? And if he was going to help me, would he expect something from me? And if he did, would that be something I'd be willing to give?

Chapter Three

"Don't leave me in here." I said softly as Tyler walked to the door of the room he'd brought me to. "Please."

"You'll be safe." He stood by the door and frowned. "He won't come in and do anything. I'll make sure of that."

"How long am I going to be in here?" I looked around the small bedroom and sighed. "And have I been kidnapped?"

"You came here of your own volition, did you not?"

"Yeah, but I—"

"So I'm pretty sure you weren't kidnapped." He opened the door. "Just relax."

"How am I supposed to relax?" I ran over to him. "Let me leave."

"No." He shook his head. "Not yet."

"When?"

"When it's the right time."

"What happened to Eugenie? I know you know." I asked him again, hoping to break through to him. I knew this was his job, but if his boss was a psycho, he had to know what he was capable of. I refused to believe that he would just leave me here.

"I don't even know who Eugenie really was." He shrugged. "Stay in the room and be quiet. I'll see what I can do."

"Why won't Grant let me leave?"

"I can't tell you that." He shook his head. "Please stay in here and be quiet. If you make a lot of noise I'll have to handcuff you."

"What?" My voice rose and he pursed his lips.

"Evie."

"This is crazy." I shouted. "I feel like I'm in the twilight zone. What's going on here?" I tried to grab his arm, but he walked away from me and out of the door. He pulled the door closed behind him and I heard a key turning. I tried to turn the handle, but the door wouldn't open. Why me? I banged on the door for a few seconds and then stepped back. I didn't want Tyler to come back and handcuff me. Then I'd really start to panic. How had I not seen that Grant was a psycho? I was so confused by everything. I just didn't understand what was going on. Why oh why had I let Hailey talk me into this? Why had I thought it would be a good idea to spend the night with Grant? What dance did I think was five grand? Especially a dance from someone like me. I went and sat on the bed and tried to think. What was I going to do now? I tried not to feel bad for myself. I knew that wasn't going to get me out of this predicament. Then I thought about what I would tell someone else to do in this situation. I wasn't an investigative reporter for nothing. I needed to find out why Grant wouldn't let me leave and what had happened to Eugenie. I decided to look around the room to see if I could find any clues. It was the only thing I could think to do that wouldn't make me feel like I was about to lose it. I knew I needed to keep my mind occupied. I looked around the room and saw a large closet and decided to explore in there first.

As soon as I opened the closet I froze. It was filled with women's clothes. Were these Eugenie's clothes? I bit my lower lip as I went through the pockets of all of the trousers. I didn't feel like I was snooping in the closet. I mean I was just looking through the clothes. It's not every day you get locked in a room with nothing to do. It's not every day that you think you've been kidnapped, even if you did go to the house voluntarily. I was searching through a pocket when I saw a stack of letters on the top shelf. My heart froze and I pulled them off of the shelf quickly. They were all stacked carefully, with a small silver paperclip keeping them together. I held them to me and looked towards the door to make sure no one was about to come into the room. I walked back to the bed and looked at the pile of handwritten letters anxiously. I stared at the first letter and immediately my eyes started reading.

The first kiss was like poison. Once I had a taste of him, I was dead. Once he had a taste of me he was crazy. We were crazy in love. We were crazy in the head. We were parasites to each other. I didn't know how to get away. How do you leave the man you love? How do you cleanse yourself of toxins when your body craves them? I don't know the answer. All I know is that I'm consumed by him.

There was no name at the bottom of the letter, but all I could think is that Eugenie must have written the letter. I eagerly placed the first letter next to me on the bed and read the second one.

He took me out today. I thought he was going to give me my freedom. I cried at the possibility of my loss. He cried too, but for a different reason. We made love in the fields. There were flowers of every color: green, red, yellow, blue, purple, and pink. They filled my every sense. I felt like I was in another world. I wanted to be in another world. I didn't want the magic to stop. I didn't want to go back.

My heart started beating rapidly as I read the letters. What did she mean by she thought he was going to give her her freedom. Had Grant kidnapped her as well? I quickly turned to the next letter.

I got high today. It felt good. I didn't tell him and I feel guilty. I think he knows though. I don't want him to know where I got the drugs. I don't want him to know what I did or my secrets. I feel dirty. But I also feel good. God help me, but I love this feeling. I'm flying so high. I'm fucking flying on a magic carpet and he's taking me to hell and back.

I shivered and turned to the next letter quickly.

Am I crazy? I lied. He lied. I want to leave before I break down. I made a mistake. I shouldn't have trusted him. He's going to be my downfall. And now it's over.

What had Eugenie lied about? Was it the drugs again? I felt frustrated reading the letters and not knowing exactly what she was talking about.

Help me. I'm scared. If you find this, please help me. I'm Eugenie Parker. I'm 21 years old and I've been kidnapped.

I dropped the letter on my lap. So it was Eugenie. I could feel my face growing hotter as my stomach started to churn, but I kept on reading.

I am I cried. I am. I'm trying. Writing in black and white is hard. He doesn't know what's happening. What's happened? I don't know if he cares. He abandoned me. I haven't left this room in three days. Help me, please. There's no magic anymore. Just me. Only me.

I turned quickly to the next letter, but it was just a blank piece of paper. All of the rest of the pages were blank. I glanced back at the letters and reread them, trying to memorize them and find clues anywhere that I could. What had happened to Eugenie? What had Grant done? How had she died? Did Tyler know what had happened? Had he been here working for Grant? Had he locked her in this room like he'd done me? Had he promised her she'd be okay as well? Had I walked into a trap? And if so, what did it mean that I was now in her room. Was I next?

Chapter Four

I woke up to someone touching my face. The room was dark and I realized I must have fallen asleep after I'd hidden the letters back in the closet. I blinked in the dark and tried to make out the face of who was with me. I let out a sigh of relief when I saw Tyler. I wasn't sure what I would have done if it had been Grant.

"Hi, how are you doing?" He asked as I sat up and looked at him.

"How do you think?" I replied in a surly fashion. I didn't care if he thought I was a bitch. He couldn't expect that I was going to act happy to see him.

"You look well rested."

"Are you going to let me leave now?"

"What if I said you could leave." He tilted his head to the side.

"I can go?"

"Do you want to go?" His brows furrowed and he gazed at me with such a sad look that I felt my heart breaking for the unspoken hurt in his eyes, What was Tyler's story? Something in me couldn't look away or talk as I stared at him. I'd never experienced such a feeling before. I felt as if I were having an out-of-body experience as we stared at each other.

"What are you thinking about?" He asked me softly as we sat in the dark room.

"Wondering how I got myself into this position." I said after a few seconds of silence and sighed as I continued to stare at him. "It's just my luck that the one guy I chose to have a one-night stand with is a psycho."

"That is a shame." He nodded.

"How could you work for him?" I asked him with a confused face. "How could you work for someone so crazy?"

"I don't think he's crazy." He shrugged.

"He had you lock me up in this room." I rolled my eyes. "He's crazy."

"He does everything for a reason."

"What sort of reason?" I had started to get annoyed and loud.

"I'll huff and I'll puff and..."

"You'll blow my house down?" I finished his sentence for him and he smiled slowly.

"You're not a little piggy, dear Evie." His voice was throaty as he grabbed the front of my shirt. "I'm planning on doing a lot more than blowing your house down."

"What?" I gasped as I fell towards him. "What are you doing?"

"I was about to kiss you, unless you wanted to leave. However, I feel like you're the sort of girl that wants to get to the bottom of this before you leave."

"Why do you say that?"

"Because you've had several opportunities to make a run for it." He paused. "I gave you several opportunities."

"I didn't realize how serious everything was."

"Did he show you his chain last night?"

I nodded without answering, my face burning with shame at how easily I'd given myself to Grant.

"Did you use it?"

"Use the chain?" I repeated dumbly. "How would we use the chain?"

Tyler stood up then and bent down and picked something up. I could see the silhouette of his body reflected on the wall behind him.

"It's long and hard and stiff, yet surprisingly supple in my hands." He said softly as he stood there.

"What are you talking about?" I looked down to his pants.

"Get your mind out of the gutter." He grinned as he held up his chain. "What do you think?"

"Oh." I stared at the chain for a few seconds and jumped off of the bed. I touched the chain gingerly, wondering how this cold piece of metal could ever be used in a loving way.

"Are you thinking about him?" He whispered in my ear as his right hand grabbed my breast.

"No." I shook my head slightly and gasped as he pushed me back onto the bed.

"Good. This is about us."

"Why did he—" I started and he cut me off his with his lips.

"Now is not the time for talking. Now is the time for loving. Now is the time for me to show you what it's like to experience ecstasy in every fiber of your being."

"What are you going to do?"

"What am I not allowed to do?" His voice was hoarse.

"Why?"

"Because that's exactly what I'm going to do."

"I can't sleep with you." I shook my head. "It wouldn't be right."

"Why not?"

"I, I..." I looked away from him and blushed. "I already slept with Grant."

"So you want to be with Grant?" His voice was a question.

"No." I shook my head and then paused. "I mean, I don't know." I shivered as he ran his fingers across my stomach.

"What are you thinking about right now?" He bent down and kissed my stomach.

"I'm thinking this is absolutely crazy. I'm thinking I need to leave." I held my breath as his tongue played in my belly button and he kissed my stomach.

"Grant thinks you wanted to have a threesome." He said softly as his tongue licked down my stomach and stopped at the top of the pants he'd given me to wear earlier.

"No, of course not." I shook my head. "I don't want that." Just because I'd thought that they'd wanted it didn't mean I did. No, not at all. Especially now that I was pretty sure Grant was a psycho. Now, I couldn't lie to myself about Tyler. I wanted him badly.

"Good." He nodded. "That's not what I want either."

"What do you want?" I looked into his eyes and searched for an answer.

"It's not about what I want." He rolled away from me and stood up.

"Where are you going?" I watched as he walked to the closet and opened it. My heart raced as I worried he would see the letters I'd put back. However, he didn't even look at the top shelf. Instead, he pulled out some knee-high stockings, a black bra, some black panties, a pair of black heels and a lace piece of material.

"I want you to put these on." He handed them to me. "And put the lace over your face."

"Over my face?"

"I want you to cover your eyes." He nodded, a smirk on his face. "I want to make sure you can't see."

"Why?" I frowned and sat up, brushing my hair away from my face as I stared at him.

"This is a test."

"A test?"

"A test to see who you really want."

"What?" I frowned. "And stop looking at me like that."

"Like what?"

"Like you can see into my soul."

"Oh, but I can Evie."

"No you can't." I bit my lower lip nervously as I touched the delicate garments he had handed me. "And I don't understand why you want me to wear these items."

"I already told you." He laughed. "It's a test. You're going to put these items on and you're going to lie on the floor with your legs in the air and wait."

"Wait for what?"

"You'll know when I'm ready for you."

"You just want me to lie there and wait."

"I want you to lie there and wait for me."

"On the ground?" I trembled, as he licked his lips.

"Yes, on the ground by the door. There's a cool breeze that comes through the door. I want you to lie there and imagine it's my tongue."

"Why?"

"I want you to lie there on your back with your legs in the air waiting to be fucked. I want your pussy to throb with sweet anticipation. I want your nipples to harden waiting to be touched. I want your stomach to churn with excitement. I want your heart to beat fast with every sound you hear. I want your body to experience the exhilaration of not knowing what's going to come next."

"Then you're going to touch me?" I whispered and stared at his lips. How could I say no to him when I was already wet?

"I'll only touch you, if it's me you want."

"What?"

"As you lie there waiting, your body will tell you who you're craving."

"How?" I asked him stupidly. I already knew who my body was craving, though I didn't understand how I could want to be with Tyler so badly.

"Because when you feel the first touch of a finger or a feather, someone's face will pop into your mind. Then you'll know who you really want."

"I don't understand." I shook my head in confusion. Wasn't it going to be him touching me?

"You won't know if it's me or Grant touching you."

"What?" My jaw dropped. "I don't understand." I dropped the underwear on the bed. "Both of you are going to touch me?" I shivered. "Isn't that considered a threesome?"

"No." He shook his head. "Only one of us will touch you. You will not know who."

"I can't just lie there and wait." I stumbled over my words, excitement coursing through my body. "I can't let someone touch me and not know who."

"Why not?" He ran his fingers across my lips roughly. "What are you afraid of?"

"I'm not afraid of anything." I shook my head. "Why am I here? Am I just a sex toy? Is that why Grant won't let me leave?"

"You're here because you met Grant at a bachelor party. He offered you five grand for a dance and you slept with him." He shrugged and I could hear a tinge of anger in his voice.

"So why are you coming on to me?" I snapped.

"Because I think you made a mistake with Grant."

"Why would you think that?"

"Because you want me." He smiled smugly and leaned in. "You want me to fuck you so badly, I can see it in your eyes."

"No, I don't." I swallowed hard. "Where's Grant?"

"Do you really want to be with him? Didn't you say he was crazy?"

"No, you said he was..." My voice trailed off. "I want to know what happened to Eugenie."

"Why?" His face turned to stone. "I told you earlier that—"

"I don't care what you told me earlier." I shook my head and then gazed at his hands as he pulled some pearls out of his pocket. "What are they?"

"I want to put them around your neck." He smiled. "Maybe you'll find out what else they can be used for later."

"Will you tell me about Eugenie?" I asked softly. "I don't need to know what happened to her. You don't have to tell me what happened, I just want to know about her."

"Is that why you haven't left?" He ran his fingers across my lips. "You want to get to the bottom of her story, don't you? Even though, you have no idea who she is."

"I want to know what happened to her, yes."

"And you want to fuck me too, don't you." He pushed his finger into my mouth and I sucked on it gently before biting down with my teeth. "Do you wish that was my cock in there instead?" He whispered in my ear.

"You'll just have to wait and see." I licked his finger delicately while staring at him and his eyes never left mine.

"I told you what happens to little girls that play with wolves." He said hoarsely and then I smiled at him.

"There's one thing you forgot to take into account." I said softly, my heart beating fast. "I'm not Little Red Riding Hood and I'm not a little girl. I'm a wolf hunter and when I get one in my grip, it's very hard for them to survive." I moved my lips to his cheek and gave him a quick kiss before moving to his ear and whispering. "In a game of predator and prey, it's not always the predator that comes out on top." I could feel my heart racing, as I played his game and his hand immediately fell to my ass as he held me against him tightly. He turned slightly and his eyes looked black in the poor light, before he turned to whisper in my ear.

"I don't care who's on top, Evie." His tongue licked my ear. "I just care that it's me you're thinking about when my hard cock is inside of you." He grabbed my hand and placed it on his hardness. "I want every long hard stroke to make you think of me." My fingers gripped his hardness and I swallowed as he grew even harder in my hands. "Now take your clothes off, put on the panties, bra and blindfold and wait. Don't touch yourself either. I want your body waiting in sweet anticipation for the moment when one of us touches you."

"I don't want—" I started, but he cut me off and stepped away from me.

"Legs in the air, Evie. You'll find the not-knowing when or who will make it, even more exciting." And then he walked out of the room, leaving the door open. I stared at the open door and then at the underwear he'd given me. I couldn't believe that I was even contemplating staying; especially after seeing the letters and being locked up in the room. However, I just couldn't seem to leave. Not yet. I wanted to see how everything was going to play out. I wanted to find out exactly what was going on here. And if I was honest with myself, I wanted to be with Tyler as well. I didn't think about that too hard though as I didn't know what it said about me.

Chapter Five

Tyler was right. The anticipation of not knowing what was coming was exciting and scary. As I lay on the carpet by the door, I felt self-conscious in my bra and panties. I also wondered what the fuck I was doing lying here. I have to admit that a part of me felt like a fool. I mean, how can you not? Here I was, practically naked, with my legs in the air, waiting for someone to come and touch me. Yes, it was the sexiest situation I'd ever been in, but it was also one of the dumbest. I know some people would wonder why I stayed then. They'd ask, like Hailey, what happened to my brain? What can I tell you? I don't know. Maybe the endorphins that were rushing through my body were warping my mind. I don't know. I can't explain it. My brain was shouting at me to leave, but another part of me - the daredevil part - didn't want me to leave. The daredevil part of me wanted to see what was going to happen. The confident part of me felt like I could get through this. It was almost as if I had something to prove to myself. I wanted to get to the bottom of the Eugenie mystery and I wanted to work out Tyler's story. I knew that wanting to sleep with Tyler wasn't something I could control. It was my body, it was my soul. There was a deeper story to Tyler. I could see it in the sadness of his eyes. I could hear it in the hesitation in his voice when he spoke about Grant. I could feel it in the way his fingers touched me tenderly. Something in him struck a chord in me.

I heard the footsteps coming towards me and I froze. All of a sudden, I wasn't as excited. All of a sudden I was tense. I couldn't see anything though the blindfold. I'd have no idea who was touching me. It was a weird situation to be in. It was scary, but it was also exhilarating. A part of me had always wanted to explore my sexual side, but I'd always held back. I wasn't sure why. I wasn't sure if it was because I was sexually repressed or just scared what society would think of me. So I'd always been the good girl. I'd stuck to only sleeping with the guys I'd dated, even when they hadn't been great in bed. Even when I'd been propositioned by men so hot, they'd melted my panties off with a look. I hadn't slept with them because I wasn't a one night girl. I wasn't a girl who fucked, just to fuck. Though that had obviously changed now. I'd slept with Grant and I'd enjoyed it; psycho or not. However, in this moment, all I could think about was Tyler. I wanted to touch him. I wanted to be touched by him. I wanted to feel the electricity coursing through our bodies as we made love. I wanted to be taken to the top of the cliff, not knowing if I would make it down alive. I wanted to jump off of a building, not knowing if a net was waiting there to catch me. I wanted to be consumed by him. My body felt feverish just thinking of him. And then I felt the first touch. Right in the middle of my legs. The fingers rubbed me gently back and forth and my entire body shook immediately and I felt the pressure against my clit. I felt the fingers moving back and forth gently and then more roughly, as if they knew how close I was to an orgasm already. My legs fell to the ground and he growled and pulled them back up. I moaned at the loss of his fingers and felt him move my legs over his shoulders. He leaned down and kissed me gently on the lips.

"Tyler." I said gently, knowing it was him from his taste and smell.

"You saw me?" He responded as he pulled the blindfold off of me.

"No." I licked his lips as I shook my head.

"How did you know it was me?" He looked at me with surprised eyes.

"I knew your smell. I knew your taste. I knew your touch." And then I said the words I'd been thinking from the beginning. "And I knew it was you that would come."

"Oh?" His eyes twinkled. "You knew huh?"

"I knew." I nodded. I knew deep inside that there had been a little bit of doubt, but internally I'd known, somehow, that it would be him that came. I wasn't sure I'd have been able to sit and wait if I'd thought there was a real possibility that Grant was going to come.

"You sound very confident." He smiled.

"Was there a possibility that Grant was going to come?"

"Grant went out, so no." He paused. "Not this time."

"Not this time?" I raised an eyebrow at him.

"How do I know you won't change your mind and want him instead of me?" He stood up and pulled me up with him.

"I'm not that sort of girl." Even as I said the words, they sounded false after everything that had happened.

"What do you want to happen tonight, wolf hunter?"

"I don't know." I whispered as his fingers ran across my shoulders.

"Touch me, tease me, and never leave me. Kiss me, lick me, I won't think you're easy. Fuck me, blow me, and close your eyes. I'm going to take you on the ride of your life." He whispered in my ear as his fingers trailed down my stomach and closer to my panties. "Do you like this, Evie?" His voice was raspy, more urgent and his eyes searched mine. I stared back at him with my heart pounding. I shivered at the look of desire in his eyes. I was in over my head and I knew it. He smiled then, a warm satisfied smile as if he could read my mind. His fingers stopped their journey and he grabbed my hands. "Are you ready for what's next?" He pulled me closer towards him, not blinking. I nodded slowly, barely believing that I was actually in this situation and agreeing to his unspoken offer.

"Good." He said before his lips crushed down on mine, claiming what was his. I melted against his chest and kissed him back passionately. Wanting to be an active part of this journey he wanted to take me on. His hands squeezed my shoulders as he kissed me and I cried out as he pulled my hair roughly. He chuckled at the sound and pulled away from me. "You need to toughen up if you want to do this. Do you understand?"

"Yes." I finally whispered a reply. "I understand." Though I really wasn't sure what he meant by toughen up.

"I like you Evie. I really do." He said as he reached behind me to undo my bra.

"You don't even know me." I whispered as I felt my bra being thrown onto the ground.

"I know everything I need to know." He took my hand and guided me to the bed, pushing me down before straddling me. "I know that you taste like honey." His lips found my right breast and he sucked on my nipple eagerly as his hand played with my left nipple and rolled it around in his fingers. His teeth gently tugged my right nipple and I squirmed underneath him as I felt ripples of pleasure coursing through my body. His tongue flicked my nipple back and forth and then he looked up at me as I moaned. "I expect you to be louder when I'm eating you out." He grinned and kissed down my stomach, before pulling my panties off.

"Oh." I felt delirious at how fast everything was moving. His face was in my wet pussy before I could blink and I felt him sucking on my clit before gently flicking it with his tongue. My body moved of its own volition underneath him and he lapped my juices up eagerly before pulling away.

"What are you doing?" I moaned as he rolled to the side of me. I looked over at him and sighed. My body felt cold and empty without him on me and touching me.

"I told you I wanted to hear you be louder when I ate you out." He licked his lips as he stared at me. "You taste so fucking good." He grunted as he licked.

"I was moaning." I whimpered and reached out to touch his chest. "Don't stop."

"You weren't loud enough for me." He lay back and I stared at his chest. "I couldn't tell that you wanted it."

"What do you want from me?" I whispered as I stared down at his face.

"You tell me Wolf Hunter." He winked and I knew that this was a challenge. Once again he was testing me to see how far I'd go. I grinned down at him as I felt a surge of energy and power coursing through me.

"Okay." I grinned and stood up. I saw the hesitation and worry in his voice. He thought I was going to leave. That made me feel even more confident as I pulled his boxer shorts off.

"You do that like you're a pro." He grinned as he realized I was staying.

"I don't know that that's a joking matter." I shook my head with a smile before taking his cock in my hands and running my fingers down his shaft and grabbing his balls. "I don't know if you want to play with me right now."

"Oh?" He grunted as his body froze.

"I think..." I paused and bent down. "I think you should be very careful with your words right now." I took his cock into my mouth and sucked hard, bobbing up and down for about a minute as he groaned beneath me. I could hear his breathing growing harder as I took him deep into my throat and then sat up.

"What?" He muttered as I sat on the bed next to him.

"Yes?" I smiled sweetly and then yelped as he pushed me back onto the bed and got on top of me.

"You want to play games with me?" He grunted in my ear as his fingers slipped between my legs and entered me. "Do you think you can win?" He kissed my neck as my body convulsed beneath him. "Do you think you can tease me and not give me what I want?"

"What do you want?"

"I want you, Evie." He grunted in my ear. "I want to please you. I want to touch you. I want to taste you. I want to save you."

"Save me from what?" I gasped as his fingers rubbed my clit rapidly, bringing me to the edge of orgasm.

"I want to save you from yourself." He grunted as I exploded beneath his fingers, my juices flowing into his hand and over his fingers. My back arched and I screamed at the intensity of my orgasm. My whole body was shaking as I lay there and he kissed me lightly on the lips. "Did you enjoy that?"

I nodded and then pushed him back and straddled him, rubbing my juices over his still hard cock and thighs.

"Hold on." He reached down and grabbed a condom packet and I moved over as he slid it on. His eyes never left my face as he guided my hips back over to him. I moved forward and felt the tip of his cock rubbing against my entry. I moved forward gently and he grabbed my hips and lifted me up slightly and then sat me down. I felt his cock filling me up and I started to move back and forth quickly, my mind on nothing other than making him come as hard and fast as he'd made me come. He grabbed my breasts and played with my nipples as I rode him hard and fast. I could feel that I was going to come again and he could sense it as well. He grabbed my hips and moved me faster, all the time grunting as his cock slid in and out of me.

"Come for me, Evie." His voice was hoarse. "Come for me."

I screamed as I felt his finger rubbing my clit as I continued to ride him. My orgasm was even more intense this time and I could tell from the shaking and then stilling of his body that he was coming as well. I collapsed on top of him and I could feel tears rolling down my eyes.

"Are you okay?" He wiped my tears away and then kissed me.

I nodded slowly, knowing that a part of me was forever changed. That I could never go back from this moment – because of my actions from the last two days.

"Good because I want to fuck you again." He grinned at me. "I'll give you a few seconds to get ready."

"A few seconds?" I smiled at him and looked into his eyes, my heart beating fast. I still felt slightly concerned at my situation. I still felt like I was in a dangerous situation. I still felt every nerve in my body on edge.

It was then that I heard the door close, and footsteps walking back down the corridor. We hadn't been alone. I shivered at the thought. Had Grant been watching us?

"He knows?" I looked up at Tyler in confusion, anxiety running through my veins.

"Yes." He stilled. "He knows."

"Why was he watching us?" I asked softly, cuddling into him to keep warm.

"In case you wanted him." Tyler whispered against my head. "And in case you were still lying on the ground waiting." His fingers ran down my back. "You see Evie, I just made it to you first."

Chapter Six

I stared at Tyler with a shocked expression as my stomach dropped. "What do you mean you made it to me first?"

"I'm joking." He sat up and pulled me up with him. "There was never any possibility of him touching you again."

"What do you mean?" I shook my head and felt my hair cascading down my back. "You just said…"

"Grant's not going to touch you again." He said firmly. "You're mine now."

"I'm yours?" I could hear a bell ringing in my ears. "And Grant was okay with that?"

"I've got things on him." Tyler shrugged.

"So I can go?"

"He doesn't want you to leave yet." He shook his head and sighed. "This is a delicate situation."

"Why?"

"I'm not in a position to say." He leaned forward and kissed me.

"Does it have to do with Eugenie? And her death? Does it have to do with the drugs he gave her?"

"What drugs?" He froze and looked down at me. "What drugs?" He said again, this time his voice rising.

"The drugs that made her think she was losing her mind." I bit my lower lip and tried to remember my training. What was I supposed to do and say in a situation like this? I froze as I realized I had no idea. I wasn't a real investigative reporter. I was just a wanna-be and none of my classes had prepared me for a situation like this.

"How do you know that she took drugs that made her lose her mind?" He ran his hands through his hair. "What are you talking about?"

"I found some letters." I took a deep breath, not sure if I could trust him, but knowing I didn't have much of a choice. "She wrote letters."

"She did?" His eyes widened. "What did they say? Where are they?"

"In the closet." My heart thudded. "What did Grant do, Tyler? Why are you working for him?"

"It's complicated Evie. Please show me the letters. Did they mention, Grant?" He asked softly.

"No, she never named him." I bit my lower lip and walked over to the closet and pulled the letters out. "She loved him, but he lied to her about something. She was also on drugs. She seemed like she was losing control."

"Let me see them." He grabbed the letters from my hand and walked back to the bed and turned the lamp on and read them quickly. He placed them on the bed next to him and I could see that he was deep in thought.

"What are we going to do?" I asked as I walked towards him. He looked up at me with a distant look in his eyes. He stared at my body from head to foot and stood up and grabbed my hands without speaking. "Tyler?" I asked hesitantly. "What are you thinking?"

He pushed me down onto the bed, his eyes searching mine before kissing me hard, his tongue taking control of mine as he sought refuge in my mouth. His hands reached down and spread my legs and he positioned himself on-top of me, his cock resting next to my pussy. His lips moved from my mouth and down my neck, nibbling everything they touched. He grabbed my arms and pushed them up above my head held them back tightly.

"Tyler?" I said his name again, my body on high alert. He grabbed something from the table next to the bed and I only knew it was handcuffs when he slid one side over my wrists and attached it to the bed post. "Wait, what are you doing?" I asked and closed my eyes as his blue eyes blazed into mine. Still he didn't talk. He turned off the light and reached for another condom and slid it on his already hard cock. His fingers played with my nipples as I lay there, trying to move my arms, even though I wasn't able to. He laid back on-top of me and kissed me lightly. I felt the tip of his cock at my entrance and his eyes sought mine. I nodded slightly and he entered me hard and fast. I moaned as he slid into me, filling me up. I wanted to reach out and grab him, but I couldn't touch him.

He sat up slightly and pulled my legs over his shoulder, his eyes filled with desire as he looked down at me. He slammed into me over and over again, his balls bouncing off my pussy as his cock claimed me. My body couldn't stop from trembling and I felt him stilling inside of me as he climaxed. He stared down into my face as we both came.

"I want to erase every memory of Grant from your mind." He said quietly as he collapsed on top of me.

"I'm not thinking of him." I shook my head.

"Why are you here with me, Evie?" He sighed and played with my hair. "Why did you come here?"

"I told you why." I sighed and looked at him. "Maybe I was an idiot, but it's too late for me to have any regrets."

"Why did you cry earlier?" He asked softly as he undid the handcuffs.

"I don't know." I looked away from him. "Maybe at the loss of my innocence."

"You were a virgin last night?" He looked skeptical.

"No." I laughed slightly. "No, I wasn't a virgin, but I also wasn't someone that had one night stands. I don't go from bed to bed." I stared at him. "But I can't say I would blame you if you didn't know that."

"My sister died of a drug overdose." He sat up and crossed his legs as he changed the subject.

"Oh?" I sat up as well and brushed my hair out of my eyes. Was this why he'd gone quiet?

"I didn't know she was on drugs when she died." He ran his hand over his head. "I mean I knew she'd done drugs. I thought she was clean when she died. I thought I'd helped her."

"How did she die?" I asked softly.

"How did she die?" He repeated my words softly. "She died from drugs. A broken heart. Desperation. She lost her way." His voice dropped. "Sex, drugs, and rock and roll. Not always in that order and not always fun."

"I'm sorry." I grabbed his hands and rubbed his palms in mine. As we sat there in silence I realized how odd this moment was. I was sitting naked with a man I'd met the day before, comforting him. Though that wasn't the oddest part. The oddest part was that I felt like I was meant to be here. The oddest part was that my whole being felt like my life had been building up to this moment and this man. This man I'd never met before yesterday.

"You ever feel like there's one moment in your life that defines you? One moment that will change the path of your life forever?" He sighed and I nodded. I knew exactly what he was talking about. "My sister's death was that moment. When she died, I vowed that I'd be a different person. I vowed that I wasn't going to let society dictate the way I lived my life."

"Is that when you went to work for Grant?"

"Grant's not the man you think he is." He looked into my eyes. "He's not the guy I thought he was."

"We should leave. We should report him." I said earnestly. "We don't have to stay here. You don't have to work for him."

"I can't leave, Evie." He shook his head. "You can't leave. Don't you understand?"

"Understand what?" I exclaimed. "I don't understand what you want me to understand."

"You don't get to just come here and leave. Grant chose you for a reason."

"What do you mean?" I shivered and pulled my hands away from him. "I'm not with Grant anymore."

"You came here with Grant." He sighed. "He has a plan for you."

"What plan?"

"It's not for me to say." He shook his head and stood up. "I should go."

"Where are you going?" I whimpered, not wanting to be left alone.

"You trust me right?" He pulled me up towards him and kissed my lips.

"I think so." I kissed him back softly.

"I can't just change how everything operates Evie. There's a plan in place. Grant is the one that makes the decisions."

"But you said I'm with you now."

"He won't touch you again."

"What will he do then?"

He looked at me silently and then turned his head to the side.

"Is he going to do to me what he did to Eugenie?" I grabbed his head and turned him to look at me. "Just what have I gotten myself into Tyler?"

"Do you want to leave?" He bit his lower lip. "I can let you go now. I can let you run away."

"But what about everything?" I asked slowly as he ran his fingers down the valley between my breasts.

"Everything like what?"

"Eugenie. The truth. I could tell from the look on your face that you didn't know about the letters or that Eugenie was being given drugs." I stared at him as his face contorted. "We shouldn't let Grant get away with this."

"I don't know what happened with Eugenie."

"Don't you want to know the truth?" I took a deep breath. "I don't want this—"

"Are you prepared for what happens if you stay?" He cut me off and pulled me towards him urgently. "This isn't a game Evie. This is real. There's a possibility that..." His voice trailed off and he shook his head. "No, you should leave. I want you to leave."

"What about Grant?"

"What about him?"

"Won't he ask where I went?"

"I can deal with him." He pulled me towards him and hugged me tight. "There's a woman that once told me that you are what you are and you only are if you do and if you don't do then you're nothing."

"What?" I frowned, confused by his words.

"There's nothing more important to me than you leaving here safely." He stroked the top of my head. "Unless you think you can handle staying."

"What do you mean?"

"If you stay..." He paused. "There are things that you might have to do."

"What sort of things?"

"I don't know." He grabbed my hands and pulled me towards him and whispered in my ear. "There are things you might have to do that might make you uncomfortable."

"What?" I asked and I felt his hands digging into my side hard.

"Don't move." He whispered again. "He's back."

I didn't need to ask who. I froze as I heard the door open slightly. The room was dead quiet as we all stood there waiting for someone to speak.

"Someone found her wings." Grant's voice was husky and I heard the rustle of chains in his hands. I stood there next to Tyler and shivered as his grip tightened.

"Can we help you, Grant?" Tyler's voice sounded stiff.

"I thought we could all play a little game." Grant walked towards us. "What do you say, Evie?"

"What?" I turned around slowly, trying to cover my body from him and he laughed.

"Why are you being modest?" He frowned. "It's not as if I haven't seen it."

"Grant." Tyler's voice was angry.

"I know you're not getting angry at me." Grant snapped and held his chain up. "I found her Tyler. She's mine."

"She doesn't want to be with you, Sir." Tyler took a step towards Grant.

"Let's play a game and see." Grant smiled at me. "What do you think Evie?"

"What game?"

"We're not playing any games?" Tyler took another step forward.

"Why not?" Grant's smile dropped. "You never minded the games before. In fact, I thought you quite liked them."

"What games?" I asked again, my head feeling heavy.

"We can go in the hot tub." Grant said again. "Tyler likes the hot tub, don't you Tyler."

"Fuck off." Tyler growled.

"Should you really be talking to me that way, Tyler?"

"Evie found some letters." Tyler said softly. "Letters written by Eugenie."

Grant's eyes narrowed and he stared at me. "What did they say?"

"What did you do to her?" I said loudly. "What are you trying to do to me? Why won't you let me leave?"

"This is a game." Grant frowned. "This is just a game."

"A game where she can't leave?" Tyler grabbed my hand. "Why did you—"

"Where are the letters?" Grant looked around the room.

"I want to know what happened to Eugenie!" I screamed out in frustration and both men turned to look at me. I stood there and I could feel my body regaining strength and power. "What the fuck is going on here?"

"You want answers?" Grant said softly and I nodded. He smiled for a few seconds and then took a step towards me. "What else do you want, Evie?"

"Excuse me?" I said, my breathing coming hard.

"What else or who else do you want?" His eyes surveyed my body and I could feel my nipples hardening involuntarily. Why was my body still reacting to him still?

"Grant." Tyler's voice was husky as he stood next to his boss. He looked at me then and surveyed my naked body in silence. I stood there frozen to the spot, my heart racing and my head spinning. Both men were in front of me, looking at me with questions in my eyes. All of a sudden I didn't know which way was left and which way was right. All of a sudden the room felt a lot smaller and a lot darker. All of a sudden both men suddenly appeared a lot larger and more dangerous than before. As I looked back and forth at Grant and Tyler's faces I wasn't sure which one to trust. Or if I could trust either of them? Was this all just some elaborate game and plan to them? Was I really safe with either of them? My head pounded as I stood there thinking about everything that I knew. I really had no reason to believe that either of them had my best interests at heart.

"Let's see what Evie wants, Tyler." Grant's voice was low and he had a snarl on his face as he stared at me. In that moment, he looked very much like the wolf Tyler had called him.

"What I want?" I swallowed hard as he reached out and touched my shoulder. I took a step back and Tyler took a step towards me and touched my other shoulder. I felt both of their hands massaging me and I melted a little inside.

"What do you want Evie?" Tyler's voice was rough and he wouldn't make eye contact with me. I felt his hand slide down to my lower back and I froze and turned to look at him. He finally turned towards me and I could see a look in his eyes. I knew from his look that this wasn't a part of his plan. This wasn't something he wanted to happen.

"What do you think I want?" I asked softly and froze as Grant's hand moved to my ass and squeezed it softly.

"I know what I want." Grant whispered in my ear. "And I think you want it too." His finger slipped in-between my legs and ran up my butt-crack lightly, before going back down and rubbing me between the legs. My body reacted immediately to his touch and I trembled for a few seconds before stepping back.

"Don't." Tyler stepped forward and pushed Grant back. "Don't touch her."

"But..." Grant frowned and Tyler grabbed him and they left the room. My body was trembling in shock as I realized how close I'd come to being in a situation that left me breathless and confused. I quickly grabbed the clothes I'd been wearing, before Tyler had given me the sexy underwear, and pulled them on. I heard Grant and

Tyler arguing as they walked down the corridor and I stood in the doorway and waited for them to be out of sight. There was no doubt in my mind now. I wanted to leave. I didn't care what connection Tyler and I had. This was just a little too much for me. I was finally coming to my senses and I knew that this was not the place for me to be. I didn't even care about finding out how Eugenie had died. I was past the detective mode stage. I could still feel Grant's fingers between my legs as Tyler massaged my lower back. I'd been this close to doing who knows what. I felt like I was going out of my mind. And I needed to leave.

I ran down the corridor to find a way to escape when I heard the footsteps coming back towards me. "Shit." I muttered to myself and opened the door to my right. I ran inside the room and looked for a place to hide. I saw a closet and ran towards it quickly and opened it quietly and stood there with my heart beating fast. I kept the door slightly ajar so that I could try and see what was happening. I felt like I was going to have a heart attack or a panic attack. I was so scared and confused. And then they stopped right in front of the door. I watched Tyler and Grant standing there looking at each other furiously and I closed my eyes. If they came into this room, I'd be found. If they came into this room, I would be the wolves' dinner.

Chapter Seven

"Why did you touch her?" Tyler's voice was angry. "What were you thinking?"

"I thought you wanted us to test her, to see how far she would go." Grant's face twisted. "Isn't that the test?"

"This was different."

"I don't know what's changed." Grant blinked.

"You don't need to know, Sir."

"You're overdoing it now, Tyler. There's no need to call me Sir." Grant looked annoyed.

"That's how a driver would address his boss, is it not?"

"I'm not your boss."

"You know our arrangement, Grant."

"It just feels weird." He sighed. "I don't know, I think we should just let her leave. She's finding out too much information."

"You gave Eugenie drugs?"

"What?" Grant swallowed.

"Her letters said you gave her drugs."

"It was..." Grant sighed. "I didn't even know Eugenie wrote any letters." He bit his lower lip. "Why did you tell Evie about her anyway?"

"That was a mistake." Tyler clenched his fists. "But that's why she has to stay." Tyler's voice was hoarse. "We can't have her knowing too much. What if she found something else and didn't tell me?"

"I don't think this is a good idea." Grant sounded angry. "I think we should just let her go."

"I'm not done with her." Tyler's voice was loud and in control, but I could hear his anger. "And what I say goes, remember?"

"I thought I was in charge?"

"You thought a lot of things, Grant. But your time is over. If you want to continue getting paid, you'll do as I say. Evie stays and I want you to keep the fuck away from her."

"She'll never choose you over me." Grant sounded pissed. "Especially not when she hears the truth."

"What truth, Grant?" Tyler's voice was soft as he spoke and he looked at Grant with a deadly expression. I wanted to step out of the closet so I could see them better and ask them what this was all about, but I didn't move. Something told me that I hadn't heard everything yet.

"Once she knows that you're the billionaire and not me." Grant licked his lips. "And once she knows that Eugenie was your ex, not mine. Once she knows, it'll be over for you."

"And why do you think she'll find that out?" Tyler took a step towards him and I held my breath. If he looked to the right, he might see me. I knew that if he saw me it would all be over for me. I knew he'd see the shock in my face. I knew he'd see that I was devastated. He was the billionaire? He was the one that had dated Eugenie? Why had he been trying to help me escape then?

"Because I'm going to tell her." Grant's voice boomed. "I'm going to tell her that it was your decision to keep her here. I'm going to tell her that it was you that wouldn't let her leave."

I stepped back and put my hand over my mouth in fear. I'd been duped. Well and truly duped and I had no idea what I was going to do. My whole body froze in fright as I realized I could hear the breathing of another person next to me.

"Don't scream." A soft voice whispered. I bit down on my hand to stop myself from screaming, but I knew that I was minutes away from collapsing. "You have to be quiet or they'll know we're here." She whispered ever so faintly. "And if they know that you know the truth, you'll be stuck here forever, just like me."

"Who are you?" I looked slowly to the right and my heart stopped beating as I saw her delicate features and blonde hair. I didn't need her to answer to know who she was. I was hiding in a closet with Eugenie. The Eugenie I'd been told was dead. The Eugenie that had made this mad house, now turn even crazier. I closed my eyes and tried to breathe slowly as everything started to fade. All I could think was what were the two wolves planning to do next?

Note From Author

The End of Alpha Billionaire, Part II. Thank you for reading Alpha Billionaire Part II. The final part in the serial is Alpha Billionaire, Part III and is now available for preorder for $0.99. The price will go up to $2.99 one week after release, so it's best to preorder it now! You can **get your copy here**!

To be notified as soon as I have teasers or part III is released **please join my mailing list**. You can also like me on Facebook here. If you enjoyed part II, please leave a review for me and recommend the book to your friends.

I also have an upcoming standalone book called One Night Stand that you can preorder!

Other Books By Helen Cooper

The Ex Games
The Private Cub
After The Ex Games
The Love Trials
The Billionaire's Baby
New Beginnings
How To Catch A Billionaire

Books written by Helen Cooper under J. S. Cooper include:

Rhett
Everlasting Sin
Finding My Prince Charming
The Forever Love Series
Scarred
Crazy Beautiful Love

Made in the USA
San Bernardino, CA
31 January 2016